To all those who have freed me

Green light

Julie ran through the field. She was trying get away from her parents as quickly as possible. They kept arguing over something that didn't matter, and Julie had to start running through the big open field to stay sane. She wanted to take her baby brother with her, but he was sat crying in his stroller between their two parents and she knew that she wouldn't be able to outrun them with him in his arms.

She ran free, she was running faster than she had ever had in her entire life, and her parents were calling after her. First her mother and then her father, the latter first out of obligation and then quickly out of concern because it was becoming clearer with every step that Julie wasn't turning back.

She ran through the field, a big open field of short-cut grass, the kind you could find all over the country and perhaps all over the world. Julie thought she could get from one field to another in another part of the world if she could just run fast enough. If she could just not slow down at all.

Her parents kept calling her, and Julie kept smiling—grinning, because it was only making her go faster and faster. There was no one else in the field in front of her, and no one else it seemed in the smaller field ahead of her that was separated by a wide dirt path. Julie felt like she could run around the world and get back to her parents and her baby brother before her mom and dad could even make it halfway through the first field.

A fairie flew past her like a dragonfly on steroids, and though it left a light purplish pink trail in its path Julie had no time nor inclination to look over at it. She was heading to the second field, and she was about to leap over the dirt path.

She jumped! And landed just a bit before the next stretch of grass began. This did not dismay her. She just kept running! And smiling, and she heard a dog start barking at her instinctively from the parking lot some eight-hundred feet away from her to her left. The parking lot was for a BIG building that had an indoor water park that was CLOSED today even though it soo hot and it was LABOR day so Julie thought that they would be working today out of all days but the nice boy at the front desk said something about not having enough life to guard the pools and her parents had gotten so angry and her baby brother had started crying and the boy tried to make Julie's dad happy by giving him a free swim diaper but her dad didn't need a free swim diaper he could pay for one! Besides he was too big to wear a diaper and Johnny was too small to get in the water anyways, and they had left the big butt building and there were other kids who were in the lobby and they were so sad and loud staring at the amazing indoor water slides from the big big window and Julie couldn't understand why they would be so sad when they got to see the big purple and pink slides right there (well, the pink one was actually green, but Julie thought it should be pink) I mean they were so beautiful! Julie thought and now they were in this big big big BIG field behind the building trying to have a picnic but it was too hot and Julie was too busy running!

Julie ran through the second field and saw a boy with his mom at the end of it. She slowed down as she looked at the boy. He was smaller than she was but around the same age. He wore small circular black sunglasses on his nose like certain blind mice from an animated movie. He had just picked something up from the ground, and was interrupted by the sight of the running girl. Julie slowed to a stop a few feet away from him. She was barely out of breath.

"Hi!" she said, and immediately started coughing. The boy liked the sound of her coughing. It was wet and full.

"What's your name?" she asked, wiping her mouth with one arm and then wiping the sweat off of her forehead with the other. The boy liked the pit stains on her shirt.

"Hurry!" Julie cried. "You gotta tell me your name!" She stepped up to him. "Before they get us!" She grabbed his shoulders. The boy dropped whatever the heck he was holding.

"I'm Alex!" Alex answered. "What's your—?"

"Julie! Julie, Julie, Julie. And don't you forget it, bub." She pushed Alex to the ground rather easily. Alex's mom almost started to laugh, but then her expression turned into attrition and she said, "Hey! What do you think you're doing?!" She ran up to the scene. "Who do you think you are, young lady?" she said clutching her purse.

"Hey!"

Alex's mom moved her head back in surprise/fear, and she clutched her purse even tighter.

"What's the big idea?" Julie called up to Alex's mother. "We were just *playing*."

"Yeah," Alex said, popping his head back up. "We were just—"

"Oh, shut it sweetie," Alex's mother said. Alex laid back down on the grass. He was grinning like a fool.

Alex's mother pushed a finger up on her sunglasses and looked down at this little girl. Julie followed her finger and stared right back up at her—glared at her, refusing to shield her face from the glaring sunlight.

"Now, young lady," (Alex's mother had never used this term of whatever before so many times in such a short amount of time in her entire life—she was almost conscious of it), "You can't just go around and push down whoever you'd like."

"I *don't* go around pushing down whoever I'd like, Lady. I went straight for him and pushed *him* down."

Alex giggled energetically from his supine position.

"Well—" Alex's mother reeled her head back and shook violently at Julie. "Ooooh," she said.

"Well," she started again. "You can't do that *either*." She straightened up, and pointed directly at the body on the ground. "Apologize to my son; right now."

"No!" Julie cried, as if this was the most absurd thing that she could possibly do at this moment.

"*Apologize…*" Alex's mother said through gritted teeth, "Or else you'll be sorry."

Alex giggled emphatically again. Julie thought the Lady was rather going to shatter her teeth.

"Julie!" an exasperated woman called.

"*Mom!*"

Alex shot his head back up again. He was not expecting this.

"Julie!!!" Julie's mom was wringing her hands. This looked like a situation with her daughter worse than most.

"She needs to apologize!" Alex's mother cut straight to the chase. Julie's mom, whose name was Jeanette, bent over and put her hands on her knees to catch her breath. She saw the boy sitting on the ground with his weird sunglasses lopsided and she saw Julie standing in front of him with no trace of remorse on her face or in the general vicinity at all.

"Julie…" Jeanette said, "…Just apologize to him…"

"*No!*"

"She doesn't have to!"

"Keep quiet Alex!"

Jeanette closed her eyes.

"*Please,* Julie. For me. Just, apologize. Say that you're sorry for pushing him down. *Please.*"

Julie stared at her mom being an out-of-shape woman a few yards away from her. This was the most unfair day of her life.

She turned around to the boy.

"Sorry."

"Thank you!" Alex's mother could breathe again.

"Thank you!" Alex said.

"Yeah, you're welcome," Julie said, and she turned on her heel to walk towards her mother. Jeanette reached out a hand to touch Julie as she got to her and Julie clapped her hand around Jeanette's and yanked her away from the debacle.

"Remember, young lady!" (Alex's mother had to get the last word in.) "You can't go around and just do whatever you'd *like!*"

"Yes! I can!" Julie replied without turning back. "It doesn't mean I *should* though!"

Julie and Jeanette walked back down the field towards the long-lost male family members. Alex watched them go as his own mother yanked him away. This was the best day of his life, as far as he was concerned. He was so happy that the indoor water park had been closed today!

Julie and Jeanette returned to Jack and Johnny. Jack looked up from his view into the stroller (where he was trying to figure out some fundamental truth about raising human baby boys) and he put his arms out as if to ask Jeannette, "What the hell—I mean heck happened?" Jeanette gestured towards their daughter with her free hand as her answer. Jack raised his eyebrows and sighed and ran one hand through his hair as he looked back down at baby Johnny. Baby Johnny smiled up at him, and gave him a quick squeal before turning to his left to notice his sister returning. He started clapping silently with, what was for a baby, a very serious expression on his face.

Julie and Jeanette walked up to them, and Julie looked down at her brother and gave him a quick nod of assent before looking up at her father. She squinted her eyes in the growing sunlight and put a hand up (her free one) over her face to recognize the old man. Jack looked at her and curled his mouth a little in disapproval (but only a little) and then turned and looked at the big fucking ball of fire in the sky that Julie was looking at. He closed his eyes and let the sun rays wash over him. He sighed—long and full.

He turned back to his family and said, "C'mon, let's go eat at home. It's too hot outside." He was about to add: "That's why we came to this useless water park in the first place—!" but he stopped himself for the love of his wife. (Oh, thank God he stopped himself from saying or doing things for the love of his wife.) Baby Johnny squealed again for apparently no reason, God bless him.

Jack, Jeanette, Julie, and Johnny walked/rolled back to their car, and they got in and Julie restrained herself from giving her usual criticism that they should have a bigger car now that they were a 'full family.' Her mother strapped Johnny into the booster seat, and closed his door before getting into the passenger seat in front of him. (Julie quietly unbuckled his seatbelt and rebuckled it, as was her manner, before her mother got back in the car and noticed. Johnny looked at Julie as she did it this time, and his eyes blew up in delight at the idea and reality of her sister pulling this move. Julie smiled at him before looking back down at his seatbelt, making sure it was secure.) Jack started the car and adjusted the rear view mirror for apparently no reason, and restrained himself from looking too long at his two children seated in the back (Julie sat in the middle seat, right next to Johnny). He glanced momentarily at Jeanette, who glanced back at him, and they quickly looked away from each other in embarrassment like a young couple on their third or fourth date. Jeanette held a finger up to her mouth and looked out her window as she smiled a little.

Jack drove them out of the parking lot, and the dog from before barked at Julie again as they drove past him and his owner and Julie barked back at him through the open window to say goodbye and she added another bark to the old man who was his owner and he smiled at Julie and waved to her as they drove away. Julie went back to her seat smiling.

As they turned onto the street, Jack looked behind him at the large recreational facility and grimaced in disgust at the inopportune closure of their aquatics center. And then he turned back around nearly forgetting all about it and drove them up the street to the intersection. As he got closer to it, the light turned yellow and without any choice on his part it seemed he slammed his right foot into the accelerator and flew them across the intersection.

"Jack!" Jeanette cried.

Baby Johnny caught his breath.

"Yes! That's what I'm *talking* about, Dad!

They made it to the other side just as the light turned red above them.

The Look

The boy looked at the boy with a look of pure superiority. The second boy looked at the first one and saw the Rich one. The Famous one. The Loved one. The Greatest one. He saw the Richest one, the Most Famous one, the Most Loved one—the Greatest. He saw the better one.

The boy turned away from the mirror and walked away. He heard the Voice say, "And what of you? What of all your stupidity, and your ugliness, and your annoyance, and your creepiness, and your awkwardness, and your fakeness, and your hurtfulness, and your badness, and your evilness, et cetera, et cetera, *et cetera?* You are evil boy, you are evil. You are worse than that. You are indescribably worse than that. You must be punished. You have not been punished enough. You must be punished *more.*"

"I know," the boy says, as he walks down the hall.

I know…

He heard the mirror break behind him.

Isla de Tsité

John sat in his office, and he began to remember again his time in the village. It was the happiest he had ever been, but he knew that he couldn't have stayed there and eventually he would have had to get on that plane that would take him back home one way or another. The villagers wouldn't have minded if John had stayed indefinitely and forever, in fact, they might have been happy to have a new family member like him; but somehow John knew that it would have been wrong to stay too long, and his family sure as hell wasn't going to want to move there with him.

John had a good life. He had a good family—a wife who loved him and whom he loved, three kids; one completely grown-up and independent, one finishing up college and looking for their first full-time job, one still in the midst of high school (and taking it quite hard it seemed, as if to make up for his older sisters' relatively gentle rides through school); and all three were unforgettable in their own innumerable small ways and a few big ways (John's youngest daughter, for example, was a painter, and she only seemed to be getting better and better with age). John's wife, Jia, was a schoolteacher who taught English in the neighboring city's high school (thank God for the children—especially this last one—who all attended or had attended their own city's secondary school), and John was a sales manager at a company that sold parts for water bottles and food packaging and utensils and other essential items for many families like theirs and an untold number of families who were not quite like them. John and Jia had always made sure that they and their kids had always had a life outside of work and school, and so since the beginning they had gone on many good trips together (a personal favorite of John and his youngest daughter's was Hawaii, because the two of them had gotten to see the Milky Way at night on the beach when everybody else in the family was lame and had decided to stay at the hotel) and go to the movies and go on hikes and listen to music together and whatnot and their family actually liked each other for the most part and they would speak openly with each other and even cry in front of each other and hang out and the daughters would visit often and oh it was a good life but somehow it wasn't enough. It wasn't enough.

John heard Natasha's stupid laugh outside his office and he ran a hand through his balding head. He had wanted to nail her ever since she had started working here at the company eight years ago, and there were a few times where John was sure she would have let him, but John had always resisted the temptation and stayed a good man (at least in that regard). Besides, he was even grateful in a way to Natasha for torturing him for the better part of a decade with her curves and cheap-looking business clothes, because she was the last lesson in a long line of lessons that had finally taught John that there is no rest for anybody, not even the middle class. (John and Jia had actually discussed having an open relationship years before, when all the kids were still in school, and they had agreed to try it—John, admittedly, for more reasons than Jia, Natasha sadly being one of them—but less than a week into the endeavor before any sexual contact could be made and Jia had only broken one man's heart—poor old Mr. Guo's in the science department, who mistakenly thought that Jia's new marriage update that she had confided in him at lunch one glorious Wednesday afternoon included him as a possibility, bless his lecherous soul [also, his wife was and is still very much alive—her name is Mary]—both Jia and John had agreed very emphatically that this was very weird and maybe it's just something that worked for other couples and not them and then they shook on it and almost made a fourth baby that night [if she had gotten pregnant and pregnant with another boy, Jia had said that they should name him Bin, in honor of Mr. Guo].)

John sat at his desk and sighed at his good life. He sighed again, and he was mildly getting turned on by the decreasing sound of Natasha Popov and her excessive movements outside his office. He sighed again and reached for his ergonomic elevated keyboard which he had gotten for Christmas last year from his wife (and which he loved more than just a little, having more affection for the device than some of his coworkers and subordinates and perhaps most definitely one or two of his bosses) and his gaming Alienware mouse atop his mousepad (which had a design of a cartoon mouse with shades on chilling in his hole-in-the-wall 'pad' and sipping on a cheesy looking drink given to him by his youngest daughter) which he did not use for gaming at work (John was a professional) but he did have the same mouse model back at home which he would use to conquer and divide on the PC in his and Jia's bedroom in *Overwatch* or *Dota 2* with the same buddies that he had played with as kids playing *GoldenEye* and the original *Metal Gear Solid* before further installments in the franchise made the story of the series too convoluted and, of course, drunk *Mario Kart* (especially *Mario Kart 64* and later when they were adults with damnable, lovely children and more reason to play this potent version of Nintendo, *Mario Kart Wii*) and he liked it so much that he had decided to buy the same one for his less dangerous, though sometimes just as hectic, work environment.

John moved his mouse to Microsoft Word 2021 and opened up a blank document.

A notification for a Godforsaken update popped up on his screen and John closed it with the most profound act of survival.

He began typing.

What follows is an account of my time in the village of Gilanto and the surrounding areas on the Isla de Tsité. My first indication that this was no ordinary vacation or island was most definitely the dragon. It swooped down and ate one of the villagers not 10 yards away from me on my first day there and everyone was surprised because the dragon, whose name was Benny (named after the last man he had devoured), had been going vegan for straight over a year now. The villagers were horrified, not so much out of fear, but out of anguish for their newly lost brother and out of anguish for Benny's newly lost personal cause. Lirité, my guide, turned to me as Benny flew away with a look of abject horror and pure joy on his face, and told me that he had found our first project.

The last visitor that the villagers of Gilanto had had on the island was a man named Benny. He was all about improvement this Benny, and he wanted to come here to drastically increase the quality of life for Lirité and all the other natives who called this place home. The island has slowly been deteriorating over the past century and a half (crops have been failing, animals have been dying out, even the light and colors of the sky each day have been dimming), and Benny had made it his life's new mission to try to save this place (a place which he had found on TripAdvisor and then immediately bought passage to the island[1]). Lirité told me that Benny had left his wife pregnant with their first child back at home to come here (Benny had said he couldn't bear to meet his son or daughter without first having done something to try to make the world a better place), and Lirité had hoped that after some self-perceived and perhaps some actual success here on the island Benny would change his mind and go back to his family sooner than his crusade initially permitted him. But, the poor fool never had a chance, because he had gone to the dragon's den in the mountain and tried convincing the beast to start being vegan with him (because Benny was all about self-improvement, too). Benny had done the research, Lirité said, who was present at that fateful, delicious meeting, and the campaigning buffoon had tried reassuring the dragon that his biology would allow him to be at full strength and of the soundest of mind even after cutting all the animals and cheese out of his diet. The dragon eventually seemed to agree and

---

1   The Isla de Tsité is no longer listed on the website, sadly.

be moved by Benny's moralistic arguments, but it seemed that the dragon wanted one more taste of meat before starting his new lifestyle and bent down and devoured Benny whole. Lirité said that he had given one of the biggest sighs of his life after that, and also after the dragon had burped out Benny's San Jose Sharks hat.

That's what Lirité was wearing now as he looked at me as we stood at the foot of the mountain that held the cave of Benny the Dragon. We nodded our heads at each other and began the hike up the mountain. It was very pleasant actually, like a weeklong version of Sanborn County Park to Skyline/Castle Rock, and the 6 days and 6 nights that it took us to reach the cave (which was not at the very top, thank goodness) allowed me to adjust to the more rural lifestyle of Lirité and his people. My stool only made me feel like I was at death's door on the 1st and 2nd nights, and the 5th day in the middle of the afternoon oddly enough (it might have had to do something with Lirité and I trying each other's feces and drinking each other's urine as an act of brotherhood and of survival before facing Benny when we ran out of food and were too weak from the thin atmosphere to hunt-gather up ourselves sufficient sustenances; suffice it to say, Lirité managed the experience with more grace and considerably less suffering than I). On our way up the mountain Lirité would sometimes stop us in order to point out different things to me on the island. He showed me the location of several villages that used to exist before the Zaras took them (a word in the Mronto language that literally translates to "overabundance"), and he pointed one village out in particular, the village of Mrana, which used to encompass several hills near the shores of Biscanafod (meaning "sun tears") where Gilanto makes its home. The village of Mrana attacked Gilanto when most of the other villages on the island had been taken by Zaras and had tried to conquer it, but Lirité and his father (who had been the unofficial leader of the village for many years) had acted swiftly and set fire to the hills the night of Mrana's initial attack. The Mranans had not expected such a drastic reaction from the likes of Lirité and his father, who were known throughout the island for their kindness and fairness, and after the burning had left many women and children dead and the vast majority of the huts and other structures destroyed, most of the survivors in Mrana, many of whom who had been against attacking Gilanto in the first place, Lirité would later find out, fled to the jungle in shame and were never seen again. The fighters in Mrana who stayed were steadily hunted down and killed over the course of the following week until the last 8 survivors came out and surrendered in shame and begged the village of Gilanto to forgive them and execute them. The village, who had only lost several men on the night of the first attack, were more than ready to forgive these unnecessary soldiers and accept them into their families Zaras or no, but Lirité's father had refused and in a fit of terrible fury and sorrow he slew the Mranans as they lay heads hanging on bended knees and went into the jungle that night to find the rest of them and bring them home. Lirité knew as his father entered the forest that he would never see him again.

Lirité said to me as we went up the mountain that he thought his father had spent too much of his life leading and not enough of it living. After a few minutes of silence, I asked him if he thought the Zaras had taken him, and the other villagers of Mrana. Lirité said it was possible. Very possible.

Finally, on the morning of the 7th day, we reached the Cave of Benny. I heard water dripping from the ceiling of the cave, but I don't recall seeing any drops or any water in the cave at all. Nothing touched me as I listened to the drips hit the ground and disappear into nothing. It was very cold, which is not what I was expecting for the home of such a fiery beast, and the shivering drop in temperature as we walked deeper and deeper into the cave made Lirité and I even more worried about Benny and the condition we might find him in. Lirité turned his Sharks cap backwards, and he picked up a stick from the ground and held the thick end of it so tightly I could see all the veins in his body popping out until the stick end burst into fire. Lirité held up his new torch, and I looked down and picked up what I thought was another stick by my feet but what was actually a very human leg bone. I almost dropped it in fright but my fingers gripped tightly around it and would not let go as I thought to myself that I might be holding the bone of Benny the human, the short-lived activist and my vacationing predecessor, himself.

I gulped loudly, and the gulp echoed around the cave and into the dark abyss before us. A fleet of birds flew out of the cave from its mouth two-hundred or so feet behind us. Lirité and I looked at each other, and then we turned to the darkness looming in front of us and began walking into it, fire and dragon toothpick in hand.

We walked for ages. We walked for so long that the light at the end of the tunnel behind us disappeared into darkness. We walked for so long that I forgot to feel how tired and bloody my feet had become ever since I stepped onto the shores Biscanafod a week earlier. If you had asked me then, there in the deep dark of the cave, I would not have been able to remember the concept of shoes at all. I turned to look at Lirité, suddenly remembering my brave and good companion, and I saw that his entire San Jose Sharks hat had nearly shed off. All that remained was the visor on the back of his head, hanging very lightly to his wavy hair. Lirité turned to look at me. The visor fell off.

We walked for a very, very long time. All sound disappeared for us, and all that remained was the silence of the cave. The next concept that was to go was the awareness of motion and any hope of what movement could bring. The next thing to go was Time itself. It's like we were traveling back to the very beginning. I noticed the light starting to dim. I looked over at Lirité one last time. The torch was going out… out… out… and then the light was gone.

Here was the closest I have ever been to oblivion. There, in the quiet of the cave—I thought I was about to cease to exist.

And then the eye opened. Crimson, gold. Black. The feeling of an ancestral journey from long ago began to form in me, long before the Ancients, and it began to quickly come to me—but then the other eye opened, and the dragon rushed before us in a fury of wind and heat and illuminated the cave around us with the fire and light in its body. It was Benny; great and terrible and beautiful and magnificent and utterly, utterly sad.

I looked above me, and I could see that we had reached the very center of the mountain. The chamber was huge, larger it seemed than any stadium or coliseum or pyramid that man could ever build, and yet at the very top I could still see one tiny opening like a hole poked by a pencil through a sheet of paper at the ceiling of the peak and a very small line of light coming through it. I looked back down at the dragon, and its green and red body, and I saw it turn into blue. It probably changed into many colors as we stood standing there before it, more colors than I or even Lirité could ever possibly see.

Looking into its face—and looking into his eyes—I felt that I could understand it. I think Lirité and I could both understand that Benny wanted to be better, and yet could not change his nature. I reached out a hand to touch him, and a giant tear drop fell from his eye and washed all over my hand and arm. I screamed in agony, I was burning all over, Lirité came to grab me, and the great dragon lifted his head and neck into the air and roared so terribly that it shook the entire mountain.

I looked up at him with tears in my eyes and I tried to tell him—I tried to tell him with my eyes and with my face and with my body and with my heart and with my soul and with my fear that it was okay. It was okay. Whatever he had done, or been, or thought, or felt, or whatever it was, it was okay. It was okay, and I would tell him if I thought any different.

Benny looked down at me, and I felt the room starting to clear and starting to cool down. The dragon came down closer to us, and he reached his head forward and I could feel its breath on us and it was the most beautiful thing I had ever felt in my life.

The dragon looked at me, it looked into my eyes, and I felt for the first time in my life really complete. I breathed out, and the dragon began to move away from me. It began to move away from me and Lirité, and it began to move its wings. It moved its wings up and down, up and down, faster and faster, and it began to rise into the air, and the wind began to blind us and rush past us. The dragon rose into the air, and Benny lifted his head up to the peak of the mountain, and we knew that he was about to breathe fire, more intensely and vastly and greatly than he had ever done before. We knew that we were going to die—or that we were perfectly safe—and it didn't matter which because we were smiling and we were happier than we would ever be because the dragon was about to be free! The dragon was going to be free! And then he began to exhale, and the fire dropped in his body momentarily, and then blew out of his mouth with the power of a thousand burning suns. It reached the top of the mountain and blew it open and the whole chamber filled with fire and the force blew us back down the tunnel and out of the mountain. The last thing I saw was Benny's whole body being engulfed by fire, from both without and within.

The next thing I remember I was in Lirité's arms, crying my heart out in the middle of the jungle where we had landed and being totally inconsolable. My tears washed over me, slowly healing the burns all over my body, and Lirité began kissing my wounds to make them heal faster. I had never been with a man before, though I admit I had thoughts of it, but there on the 7th day of our heartbreaking journey and on my 7th day overall on the island Lirité kissed me, and we spent the night together and our bodies took on the forms of both man and woman so that we could heal each other from the terrible and beautiful fire of Benny the dragon, the last, I had a feeling, though Lirité never said so exactly, of his kind.

The following morning we returned to the village, and Lirité's family welcomed me with open arms and all of the village of Gilanto that night mourned the loss of their brother the last meal of Benny and mourned the loss of Benny and of the human Benny and of the villagers of Mrana and Lirité's father and all the villages and groups and individuals taken by the Zaras and all those others who died before their time. I choked on my tears as we stood before the great fire on the beach, because I could really see all these people who I had never met live longer than they did. I sobbed silently as Lirité put a hand on my shoulder.

The rest of my time there was spent helping around the village and exploring the island with Lirité, my courageous guide, and one of the great loves of my life. We helped renovate huts and prepare the land for plowing. We hunted pigs and deer and fished in the ocean and in the lakes. We traveled to the tundra in the north and the desert to the south, and our bodies and breaths kept us warm and cool in turn in each harsh environment. We dove off waterfalls and risked our lives in the currents of the rivers. We traveled to the more temperate forests in the west, and crossed a grand canyon in order to reach a mountain whose peak was the highest point on all the island, save for the birds who took to the sky and laughed silently at the distance. We reached the peak in record time (in fact, it seemed our combined energies allowed us to traverse the whole of the island so fast that we were able to make it back in time for the harvest), and from the summit I looked out onto the Isla de Tsité and the horizon, the volcano created by Benny's final blast that had now gone extinct, and I imagined this is what astronauts must feel like when they look down on Earth. I turned to Lirité, and he turned to me, and we just smiled.

We returned to Gilanto in time for the harvest, and I helped as much as I could before the ship that was to bring me back to California was due to come. I sincerely exhausted myself. Breaking my back and working harder than anyone in the village or even the whole world and being totally happy for it because I must have known even then that I would never come back here.

On the last night there, after a beautiful night of celebration and feasting and dancing and music, Lirité and I sat on the beach and watched the ocean waves. After a while, I turned to my right and looked at him, and I asked him, in fairly impressive Mronto I thought, "Lirité-jan... this is a silly question... and I almost don't want to ask it, but... do you think that if Benny had survived, and if my stay here was longer... do you think that one day I could have been a Dragon Rider?" Lirité looked at me, and he thought for a moment. "Yes," he said. "I think it's possible John-jan. Very possible. But I do not know if Benny even wished to continue living anymore."

I thought for a minute or two, and then finally I said, "I think he did want to live. I think he also wanted to die; but I suppose when he let out his last breath of fire... It wasn't up to him anymore. Maybe it never was..."

The ocean waves continued moving, and they crashed quietly on the beach before us.

I heard a noise that scared me, and I realized it was my own whimpering and incoherent cries. Lirité turned to me again. "What is it John-jan?"

"I..." I said. I was shaking in fear and sadness all over. "I..." I lost my breath.

"I don't want to go back, Lirité." I turned to look at him.

"I don't want to go back. I'm too scared of... or worried about... it's too much, it's just too much over there. It's such a good life, but it's still somehow not enough."

I grabbed my head in pain, and a few tears squeezed out of my eyes and fell onto the Biscanafod between my legs.

Lirité sat silently for a long time as I tried to regain control of myself, and when I felt like I could begin to breath normally again, he said, in English: "A long time ago, when I was still a child and my father served as the guide for visitors such as yourself and Benny, a writer came to see us. He did not speak, nor did anyone ever see him write, and he would always go into the jungle and disappear for days at a time before coming back to us on the brink of starvation or bitten by a poisonous snake or with several bones broken. We would heal him, and nurse him back to health, and then the next day he would go back into the jungle again. One day, after many months of this, I was awake early one morning and I saw him heading for the trees again. I got out of my bed and rushed onto the sand to go meet him. He heard me and stopped and turned around. He looked down at me. I asked him—I did not know his name, 'Man, where are you going? What are you looking for?' He looked at me for a few moments, and then he turned back towards the jungle; and then he looked back at me. 'Tsit,' he said, and he smiled very slightly at me and went into the jungle."

Lirité sat quietly beside me for a while, remembering the man. Suddenly I remembered something. I let out a laugh.

"What is it?" Lirité said in Mronto.

"'Tsit,'" I said. That means 'bird' in Armenian. I used to date an Armenian girl in college before I met my wife. She taught me some words. That's the only one I remember. 'Tsit.'"

Lirité was smiling widely at me. The mystery from his childhood was solved. The name they had given to their home for outsiders to call it by now had more meaning to them (Lirité and his people simply called the island 'anara,' meaning 'heart.')

The tide was very quiet now. I turned again to Lirité.

"This man, did you ever see him again?"

Lirité nodded.

"Did the Zaras take him? Did he return home?"

Lirité was silent for a moment. And then he said, "He took him. We found him hanging from one of the beams of his hut one morning."

The island was very, very quiet. I looked up into the sky. The moon had disappeared behind some clouds, and it felt like I would never see it again.

The waves slowly started to move again. Somewhere I heard a seagull.

Lirité began reaching for something. "He left this note. I've never parted with it until now." He reached deep into his mouth with his right hand, so much that his arm almost up until his elbow disappeared, and he brought out the writer's suicide note. He flapped it once or twice to get the spittle off of it, and then he handed it to me. I took it, and I read it.

My eyes filled with tears, and I scrunched up my face. I began to shake all over again. I gripped the note tightly in my hand and I did what Lirité must have done as a child and threw the note into my mouth and swallowed it.

I gulped, and I started to calm down. I let out a shaky breath.

"It's more than enough, John-jan."

I turned to look at him. The man I loved.

"So don't forget to breathe," he said. And he smiled at me.

We stayed at the beach for about 20 more minutes. At one point, I said, in Mronto, "I love you, Lirité," and he said, "I love you, too."

The following morning, I was on board the ship that would take me back home, standing on the deck and waving to Lirité and all the people of Gilanto as they stood on the beach waving back to me. Right before getting on the boat that brought me to the ship, I had embraced Lirité one last time and whispered in his ear, "I wish this magic would last forever." He whispered back to me in my right ear, the one he would always kiss during our late nights venturing into the island and trying to ride a buffalo on the Great Plain of Zyfoggi or tensely climbing down a deep crack in the ground to see the shimmering lights of the Wisa ("whale") Underground: "What is magic, John, if not something that only lasts temporarily?"

I let go of him after a moment and looked down to wipe away a few of my tears. I looked up again and smiled at everyone and started laughing and said goodbye to everyone again one last time. When I was already on the boat, being ferried to the large trading ship anchored about a mile away from the shore, I thought to myself, "But wouldn't that make everything magic?" I turned to look back at the island, and Lirité lifted his chin up and waved to me.

As I stood watching the island and the villagers of Gilanto get further and further away from me, I wondered if they would ever be able to have another visitor again, or if the Zaras would take all of them before anyone else even had the chance or inclination to come here. It amazed me, I thought, how this place was not more well-known and popular. How did everyone not travel here or try to at least once a year? Why would people deprive themselves of such an enchanted pilgrimage? Why had it taken me 40 years on this earth to find this place or go to it? As I was leaving it now, I couldn't shake the feeling that the island was something that I had always known about, even as a child. I just had forgotten about it for some reason or reasons until recently. My God, I thought. This might be the last view of the island that anybody ever sees. The heart of the world is always the first to go when the people bring upon themselves the Zaras.

The island began to shake, and then the ocean, and though I've never been a religious man I thought perhaps this was the beginning of the Rapture or at the very least the better, real-life version of the Kraken in the heartbreakingly disappointing *Clash of the Titans* (although maybe it's not as bad as I remember—I doubt it though). I hung onto the railing for support as the entire world shook in front of me, praying for release, and then suddenly the quake ceased—and then an instant later a powerful burst of water blew out of Benny's volcano and rained down on the entire island and even onto me and the crew members of the ship. And then a massive noise sounded in the distance, perfectly equal on both sides it seemed, and the water rose exponentially all around us as the island released its fins and began swimming away from us. I began to laugh like a madman, and pulled myself up to a standing position and climbed on top of the railing to see Lirité and the villagers, but they were already out of sight. The fins burst out of the water on either end of the shoreline, creating two tsunamis that headed towards us, and the fins began moving up and down to give the island some momentum. The people on the ship ran in the opposite direction, and the captain screamed some orders into the PA system to try to save somebody's life, but I just stood clutching the railing and looking at the Isla de Tsité in awe. The whole world could have flown into my mouth as my jaw was dropped so low.

The tsunamis merged into one unbelievably high wave that rushed towards me, and just as it covered up the view of the island behind it, like a total eclipse beginning its reign of darkness, the island rose up into my sight again, peaking over the wave, and the fins flapped once, twice, and the island flew into the air! The tsunami dropped down into the newly-created crater in the ocean right before it hit the ship and all of its precious merchandise, and I was slapped in the face and body with the most refreshing splash of salt water that anybody could ever dream of. I didn't close my eyes for a second (well, maybe for one second), and when the water was washed over me and I was lying down on the ground drenched to the bone, I sat back up and saw that the entire deck was filled with fish. I heard a noise to my right, and turned to see a crewmember a little way's away trying to slap a fish away that was flopping around on his body. Finally the fish slapped the man in the face with its tail and flew away over the deck and into the water. The man screamed a bit and went reeling back from the slap. I couldn't believe what I just saw. The fish had just *flown* into the water. I looked at all the other fish on the deck, and one by one they started to beat their fins and fly into the air and back into the water. I turned my head back up to the sky, and

I was just able to see the island's gigantic tail fly into a group of clouds and disappear.

I sat silently, with my mouth wide open again—and the wind started to pick up around me and I heard one last deafening noise and a gust of air from the sky where the island had just gone raced towards us and blew me and the rest of the ship all the way back straight to San Francisco Bay some 3,000 miles away.

John finished typing. He sat back in his seat, and breathed in deeply. He exhaled. "Whooo." He put his hands up to his eyes and rubbed his face. He patted down his hair.

He sat at his desk silently for a while, his mind peacefully clear, and after a few minutes he raised a hand up to his mouth. He hesitated for a moment, unsure of something (though he did not know what), but then after a few seconds he put his index finger and thumb into his mouth and began to reach back. He closed his eyes a little, as his hand went further into his mouth, and he was careful not to make himself gag accidentally.

After a bit of searching near his back molars and the beginning of his throat, he was able to find it. John pulled out the small piece of paper carefully from his mouth like a mother would a toy from her sleeping baby, and he quietly waved it in the air in front of him to dry it a bit. He placed the paper on his desk, right before the keyboard, and smoothed it out with his hands before taking another look at it.

John read the note. It said, "It's too much. It's not enough. I'm sorry"

John reread the note several times. After doing so, he leaned back a bit in his chair and adjusted his glasses. He looked to the side, his eyes a little downcast.

He inhaled silently and turned back to his computer. He scrolled all the way up on his untitled word document and was about to begin reading over what he had written, but then he started to feel something. It was in his chest. It was his heart maybe. John tried to clutch it, he couldn't breathe. He tried to stand up, but decided against it and tried to calm down in his seat but the pain was just increasing. It was terrible. It was awful, and then it was over. It didn't last long. John died in his chair at his desk at work.

His family found the note and what he had written on his computer, and they read it, both things, the whole thing. They thought it was beautiful, and they didn't know what to think of it at the same time. They weren't sure what to do with it, other than reread it a few times throughout their lives. They really didn't know what to do with it, although at times some of them felt like they did (almost never at the same time though). The last person in the family to read it again was John's son, on his deathbed, surrounded by his friends and family. He passed away a couple minutes after he had finished reading it. The tablet lying on his chest. His own son put it away on a shelf in the corner after he breathed his last breath. Others in the family and those who knew them or were connected to them in some way read it too. It was passed on from one generation to the next, and then to the next generation and the one after that, and so on and so on, until one day it was lost, never to be able to be read by anyone ever again. It was just gone.

No one in the family ever published it, thank God.

A Fool

On the road where we worked and made our living, I came across a traveler. He was big and cheerful, and had not a care in the world. Us workers were carrying a particular heavy load that day, and we were hurrying to get everything onto the wagons and into the caravan so that the transporters could be well on their way and not cut our pay for being late the next time we saw them.

The traveler stopped on the path right next to me just as we finished putting one of our heaviest boxes into a wagon. The big man let out an enormous laugh, and said to us, "But why are you working so hard? You'll have no time nor health left to live if you keep working so hard."

Most of the other men groaned at the vagrant and waved their hands at him in dismissal before turning to get the next box onto the wagon, but I stopped and looked at the healthy-looking fellow and couldn't help but give him a smile. I liked the man immediately, what can I say? Though I know not why.

"Well, we have to work, mister, in order to live. We'll have no time to live and no way to feed our families whom we love, though sometimes it does not show, if we do not work."

The big man let out another enormous laugh, this one even bigger than the last.

"But that is fantastic," he said. "That is surely the best thing I have heard all day. All week perhaps! Where did you get it into your head my good sir that a man has to work so that he may live and so that he can put food on the table for his family whom he loves even if he does not always show it, which is another hysterical joke altogether that I commend you for my good sir and may God bless you for your sincere delivery of said joke though we do not have the time nor the inclination to get into the humor of it just now."

I turned a little behind me so that I may find some help from my fellow workers in talking with this extraordinary fellow, but they were all busy handling the next load and a few of them were already shooting me dirty looks for not helping them and stopping to converse with this outsider.

I turned back to this jolly philosopher, whose smile was more inviting and whose eyes were becoming brighter by the minute, and said, "But sir, surely a man must work in order to survive and in order to help those he cares for survive. Otherwise he and his family will not last very long, and they will face the harshness of the world unprotected and fall victim to it?"

The man began to nod his head most vigorously and stroked his beard quite rapidly. "You are right, my good sir, about the harshness of the world. There is no doubt about that even in the most intellectual inner chambers of the hearts of even the most learned men. But, I most heartily regret to say that you are hilariously mistaken about the connection between work and survival. Take me, for example. I am clearly a vagrant (though a fairly well-dressed one, I grant you, my heroic sir), who most certainly has no job or income to speak of. And yet, I stand before you quite alive, do I not, I am most heartily afraid to ask?"

I began to stroke my chin in the manner of this un-believable traveler in front of me (though more slowly than he), and I said next, "This is true sir, you are most certainly alive," (the man smiled happily in relief and nod-ded his head a little towards my direction), "But, forgive me for saying so, but you also most certainly do not have a family—a wife, children, not even a loyal dog—that you must look after and feed?"

The man nodded his head with a smile that was threat-ening to stretch his face off his head! "Ah! How spectacular it is to be ready for a question! Almost as magnificent as not being ready for one at all! My good sir, but I do have a family. I have many wives, and many children, and many dogs even (of both the loyal and disloyal variety, quite like the wives, I must most foolishly add, hehehehe), and I am able to feed them every day with no currency or material material whatsoever save for the song in my heart and the spice on my tongue. In fact, I am feeding you and our brothers here right at this moment with this delicious *aller et venir*, though most of them are pretending not to listen."

I dared not look behind me to check the truth of his hearty accusation.

I opened my mouth to speak, quite with a large smile of my own on my face, but the man went, "And before you speak, I know already what question you are to ask," (he be-gan to giggle), "What aforementioned points you are going to bring up," (he wiped away a few big tears falling on his big face with his big hands). "You are going to ask me, 'But sir, though I envy your positive outlook on life and admire your take—which is really not my take at all, my good sir, though I thank you for saying so—on the brotherhood of man and the grand, human family, surely you will not last long in this unprotected, vulnerable position in this harsh, harsh world?'" (It is true, that is exactly what I was going to be asking to him; in fact, he asked it for me better than myself.) "To which I will reply, 'Ahahahaha-ha! You are a most wonderful and gracious comedian! A credit to your kind, and an inspiration to us all who wish to give those we meet on the road of life a good laugh or even chuckle. You see sir, for you must surely see even if your eyes do not, I will last quite long indeed even if I am to meet my end at the very end of this path here.'" (He pointed down the road to the crossroads at the end of the path, and I heard the transporters whip their horses into movement behind me and the wagons hurried off with their merchandise in that direction). "You see, I can tell already that you, my great, great, incomparable sir, will not be able to forget me for the rest of your long and happily tragic life! Though you may most certainly want to at times."

"Enough of this!" one of the men cried behind me. "C'mon, Antony, let's go get our break." The men started to walk back up the path towards the way station, kicking the dust up around them as they went.

"'Get our break.' What another beautiful, uproarious, comical, amusing, farcical, sidesplitting, rib-tickling, killing, very funny, hoot of a joke! Surely you must be training him in the divine art of comedy, my good young Shakespearian Chappelle, you."

I turned my head back to the traveler with quite a worried expression on my face (I was quite worried).

"What is this you speak of, mister? What 'end' are you referring to at the crossroads at the end of this path? How do you know your life is to stop when you reach the end of this lane?" (I gasped as I said this, and I raised a hand to clasp one of my mouths—'one of my mouths,' why did I write this? Surely I did not mean it. Or perhaps I did.)

The man was smiling silently at me. He had his hands in his pockets, suddenly. They were not so raggedy, I thought—his pockets I mean.

"My good sir," the man began. "How do we know anything? I just know."

This worried me even more. I found myself looking down at his feet. One was barefoot, and one had a decadent blue slipper on it. (Stolen or inherited, I never found out which.)

"But… do you wish to die, Man?" (I knew not what else to call him.)

"Hmm…" the man said, and he thought for a moment, stroking his chin.

"No," he said. "Not particularly, Antony."

I looked up at him.

"Then why go down the road?"

The Man just smiled at me.

"Because I want to."

"Antony!"

I turned to my right, and saw the other workers calling to me from up the path. I stared at them a while, and lifted a hand up to wave to them and I smiled at them.

I put my hand down, and I turned to talk to the man again. But he was gone.

I looked frantically around me, and realized suddenly where he would be and I looked to my left and saw him walking down the path. He was nearly at the crossroads. I heard a noise coming from his direction and getting louder.

"You fool!"

He turned to look at me, and he grinned with all of his remaining teeth and raised a hand up to wave at me. One of the wagons came back and it trampled him underfoot of the horses. The wagon screeched to a stop.

It seemed we had forgotten to load one of the crates, again.

The Astronomer

The twinkling star. It was moving in the sky in circles like a very high and very bright drone with a somewhat inebriated pilot controlling the remote, but the boy was falling asleep on the lawn and not really taking notice of these small, concentric paths that the celestial body had no right to be taking at such speed (or at all, most likely, according to most if not the whole of modern science). Perhaps it was not an astronomical wonder at all then; perhaps it really was some remarkable manmade flight of fancy after all. But no... the boy thought. No... it's a star. It was twinkling.

The boy fell asleep. When he woke up, the star was no longer moving.

Dear Nathan,

It's good to hear from you again. It's been a while since somebody words and thoughts made me smile and laugh like that. I was on the bus when I finally sat down to read your email (sorry this is going to be a really long text, like, REALLY long—but less typos than usual, I am proud to say [Look! An M dash! And brackets! I'm learning so much from you hehe]). (Oh, God, sorry about the 'hehe.' I don't like using that in my texts anymore. It reminds me of high school,
Sorry, I think one of my coworkers is throwing up or something. I'll get back to this tmrw.

I'm back. My coworker was fine. She was just having a mild panic attack. They're usually much worse. I switched over to the notes app so that I can type this on my computer because I feel like I have so much to say after I started this last night. Like I dreamed up all the things I wanted to say to you while I was asleep.
Where to begin.

Your email. Holy shit your email. There's so many things you wrote in there that I relate to. Like so many things. Like how you said every day you wind up being fake at exactly the times where you least want to be. How you feel like you're in a scene from a movie or a tv show instead of something that's real. How you feel like you're trying to convince others and yourself that you're alive instead of just living.

Dear Nathan,

I'm sorry for getting back to you so late. I tried replying to you earlier, like a week after you sent me your email (less than a week actually) but I didn't like how it was coming out. I didn't like how *I* was coming out. Or off, whatever. I tried texting you at first, but I had so much to say (I mean, I don't think anyone has ever sent me such a long email before and I doubt anybody ever will) so I switched over to my Notes app so that I can type on my computer. But I still didn't like how it was turning out, so now I'm just replying to you on email.

I read all of what you sent me, including your short story "Out by the Pool", and… I have a lot of mixed feelings about it. I mean, on the one hand, I really liked it. No, honestly, I think I loved it. But the fact that this story is about our friends/people who used to be our friends and something that happened between them at a party YOU threw at your house YEARS ago and you saw some of what happened because of all the security cameras your dad had set up around the house (which, yeah, you really should have told us about before the party started, but I forgive you), it's just… bad. I don't know Nathan, it's a really good story, but I'm relieved you're not going to publish it. I mean, how could you? It would be really unfair to everyone who mention in the story by name and of course George and especially Kavya (also, why did you change Kavya's name in the story to "Sheepla"? Is it because she's like the sheep in the story and George is the wolf? Is it a joke? I don't get it. You're weird Nathan, but I guess that's one of the reasons I like you).

Your story really worrys me too, to be honest (I gotta use that phrase less), because I remember how Kavya was back then in our first year of college. She had gotten into Berkeley, UCLA, privates out-of-state and in state too I believe but she ended up going to Ohlone like the rest of us. (I remember Vikash called it "Harvard on the Hill" lol—sorry to bring up his name 😬) I think her family was ignoring her, I don't know, she didn't really talk to me. She's the eldest child in her family too (like me, which is I think something we used to bond over) and I'm sure that didn't help matters. But I remember during that time, November/December 2018, she really kicked things up a notch. Notch*es*. She stopped hanging out with me and a bunch of other people, and I think she just shut herself in her room or at the conference room in Suju's and just studied her ass off. Hell, even more than in high school I think. I think one of the most vivid memories in my life is walking into Suju's one evening to quickly grab a drink on my way home and seeing Kavya, that tiny girl, taking up the whole conference room and long table all by herself with her laptop and backpack and a couple of textbooks. (She didn't see me, but I saw her.) I don't know how but next thing I know she's transferred to STANFORD after just one year at Ohlone and then she went on to get her master's in some business thing idk (maybe Business Administration? No, I feel like it was something fancier) and now she's working in Wall Street or something and like helping the impoverished and refugees fleeing the genocide in Myanmar at the same time?? I admit, I've been jealous of her since Ohlone (ok, fine, since high school), but when I saw on her Instagram that she had gone to Myanmar and was literally on the ground saving lives I gave up. I really hate saying this, I feel so stupid feeling this, but when I saw that picture I thought, 'Yup, there was no way in hell I was ever gonna beat her.' THAT'S what I thought. Not the fact that she was probably saving someone's life. I'm such a fucking American.

I almost wrote, "I hate myself," but I didn't. I guess I'll come back to this later, but I really don't want to.

But, ok, what I'm trying to say is that after reading your story about her and George, and remembering how she hurried back from the backyard that night at your party soaking wet saying that she had fallen into your pool and then locked herself in the bathroom… I feel so stupid, I should have asked her more about it. Because if what you wrote in your story is true, and George really did hit her and she fell into the pool when they were in the middle of having sex and taking their clothes off… Then it just makes me think, and it makes me sick to think of it but the thought feels too true: How much of what Kavya has done after that night was motivated by that night? Is she really doing the things that she wants to do? Is she really living the life she wants? Or did George fucking hitting her do something to her? I don't know, it's probably a combination of things. Real and fake; it always is, right?

And has she even told anyone about what happened to her that night? Knowing Kavya (or well, kinda knowing her), I wouldn't be surprised if she hasn't told anyone about it in all these years… Oh, I wish you would have found the footage of that night earlier Nathan, and I wish it was clearer about what had happened. If George really did hit Kavya before she fell into the water. I know you feel the same way, that you wish you had found it earlier, and that it was clearer.

And now what? What are you going to do with that footage? Are you going to keep it? Erase it? Confront George with it? You're not going to publish the story, obviously, but what the hell are we supposed to do? Fuck Nathan. This sucks.

I have to tell you something. After I read your story, I saw George. I was invited to some thing Matt was throwing, and at first I told him I wasn't going to go, I wasn't really up for it, but then I decided to go in case George came too. He did. I talked to him. It was fine, he seemed normal. (He's well into being a nurse now over at UCSF.) I mentioned the party we were at at your house all those years ago. My heart was racing. I thought I was pretty slick about it too, it sort of just happened. Somebody at Matt's thing dropped something—a rubber ball I think (a *green* rubber ball—that's not important), and I laughed hysterically for a moment and I asked George if he remembered how Kavya had pushed Vikash at your party and he had almost toppled over. George laughed and said, 'Yeah,' but that pause right before he did… and the way he stiffened up (you know how he is, he hasn't changed in that regard), and of course he didn't say anything else about the party, and neither did I—I didn't dare… I think it happened. I don't know, I think George hit Kavya that night.

But we can't be sure, obviously. I just hope if he did hurt her, physically and/or emotionally, I just hope that he apologizes to her (who knows, maybe he already has). Or maybe it's too late for an apology? Maybe he should just stay the fuck away from Kavya.

As for me, it didn't feel right saying anything more to him that night about it, and I sure as heck don't feel like talking to him about it now. I don't know, maybe it'll never come up again… I don't know, I just don't want to force things. That never seems to work out.

Ok, I feel like I should address the other things in your email. (Sorry if that sounded rude, you just wrote a lot lol. But I want to talk about it. I do.)

I see what you're saying about not being a writer. I mean, after reading, "Out by the Pool," I could really see you becoming one, but at the same time I see your point about how artists and storytellers should be able to make stuff up instead of just create autobiographical pieces. And if they're just writing about themselves, like you say you were doing in "Out by the Pool," then maybe the person/artist isn't working in the right medium. Like how some actors aren't 'real actors' and just play themselves—but I disagree with your example. Robert Downey Jr. is a fucking GREAT actor. He was MEANT to be an actor. He's a GENIUS. You are WRONG, Nathan.

But yeah, maybe you're not a writer. Maybe you're a game designer like you say (I don't really play video games, but you can bet all your microtransactions that I'll play whatever game you make one day [if you make one—no pressure]—even though I'll probably be bad at it and you'll have to come over and finish it for me and I'll just watch you play. I mean, what better way to play somebody's game than have the person who made it be right there doing it for you? Stop, don't make fun of me about the 'microtransactions' line. STOP.)

I mean…. yeah, I don't think I'm *meant* to be a social media marketer lol. I don't even like social media (except Vine, but we all know how that ended—and YouTube doesn't count). I mean… I like to make clothes, so maybe I'm meant to be a seamtress lol?

I think you're overblowing how bad working full-time is though. You're just new to it, like you said, so you'll get used to it. And I know, I know, you said you don't WANT to get used to it, but tough shit, you have to be unless you're rich. Or homeless.

As long as you're being yourself Nathan and you have a job you somewhat like and you do stuff outside of work I think it'll be fine. I mean, we did the same stuff when we were students, right? When we're fake, we end up getting depressed, like you say, and when we're real, we're ok. That applied to us when we're in school, and that applies to us now while we're working. Just get a better job lol, and one that you like more. I'm sure your customers don't like you, either lol.

Thanks for sending me the Nausicaä opening theme. I loved it. It reminded me of Mexico, for some reason. I'm definitely going to listen to it again. When the time is right. Maybe the next time I see my family in Yucatán.

The "Son of Man" painting was ok. It's cool, I guess. Thanks.

I didn't really get the Dylan Thomas poem you sent. I mean, it's pretty. I tried reading it out loud, but you know I'm not much of a reader. And the poem is about art—I got that much (I think lol). I just don't know much about art, Nathan. I don't feel qualified to comment on a lot of the things you talk about when you talk about art. That hasn't changed in our relationship lol. (Am I depressing you? I'm sorry, I feel like I'm depressing you. Lol.)

Yeah, I don't think you were in love with Kavya either. (Even though you spent all 4 years of high school trying to convince me that you were.) She is probably the "Great Crush" of your life, as you say, but I'm glad you finally see that you weren't *in* love with her. (Although the way you looked at her at your party that night when she was laughing with all of us, you, me, George, Matt, Vikash, Jora, and all of her other friends that night sitting on one of your couches in the living room—I could tell you really loved her then.)

(Yeah, I don't think I've ever really been in love either. [Actually, I broke up with my boyfriend since you sent me your email lol. You don't know him. He was nice though. I hope we stay friends.] I think I've gotten close once or twice, to falling in love [and don't think I'm talking about Matt, God no… That was just… great sex LOL].) But the boys always seemed to go away from me before anything could really happen. Maybe deep down they could tell they couldn't love me back. Or maybe real love was something too scary for them. I don't know. I didn't always use to think this way. I used to think that guys not wanting to be with me meant that there was something seriously wrong with me. Lol, does that surprise you Nathan? Hearing that from a girl? Sorry, I don't know why that sounded so bitter.

Anyways, we're 23—[yeah, you're 23 too, I checked FB]—we still have time.

Also, I love that you're still a virgin. I fucking love that. It makes me want to kiss you long and hard but then I'd be sad I wasn't your first kiss ;) That honor goes to Jora.)

I'm tired, but I want to keep writing. I feel like I'm getting close to the end of my reply. I guess the only thing I haven't really addressed is the breathing thing. OK—whoo. Here goes then:

Stop breathing. If you keep thinking about how much better you could have been in life and you're not able to breathe when you think about that—don't. Die. Pass out. Suffocate. Just die. We all could have been better, right? Yeah, maybe you've been worse than most—maybe you've been as fake and as hurtful and as hypocritical as you say (I don't really know)—but so what? Are you suicidal? Don't make me fucking think you're suicidal when you're not. It's not fair. It's just not fair. You think because we don't really talk anymore I want you to die? Well, I don't you bitch. I love you, and just stop thinking so much about how much better you could have been. Thinking too much about that is another mistake in itself. It's another flaw you can add to your stupid list of personal flaws. (I'm sorry Nathan, but I had to laugh when I started reading that part of your email. I mean, some of these things aren't even flaws. "Cheap?" "Not exercising enough?" "Bad at visualizing things?" "SOMETIMES"? Uhhh!!! You're so STUPID; you ~~cute~~ fucking weirdo.) It's still okay for you to do some things, Nathan, despite all of the 'bad things' you've done (whether you actually did them or just made them up in your dumb beautiful little head). It's okay for you to *live*. Maybe that doesn't apply to every sinner, but it applies to you. There is no question about that. No argument. Shut the FUCK up. Hehe

Alright, I think I'm done. I'll read over whatever the hell I wrote you tomorrow. Oy vey Maria, as Daniel would say. (Whatever happened to that guy? I'm too lazy to check instagram.)

Ok, I read it. That was rough. There was a bunch of shit I wanted to change/add/take out, but somehow it didn't feel right. So here it is. Here's my reply, Nathan. I love you; let's hang out during the holidays maybe. Be well.

Your friend,
Madeline Delgado

PS Listen to Delta-2 by KVP right now (don't worry, it's on Apple Music weirdo). I think you'll like it. K bye

Your Business

"Two billion, five hundred and six thousand, eight hundred and ninety-two."

Zane looked at Ted as he gave this report. Ted was totally calm, and he was waiting for his boss/friend to say something. Zane didn't really know what to say. This report was more of a formality than anything else.

"How long did it take you guys to find that out?" Zane asked Ted, smiling slightly.

Ted laughed a little. His deep, resounding laugh. It hadn't changed at all since their days as young entrepreneurs in Silicon Valley. Zane suddenly remembered the two of them opening a kitchen cabinet in their apartment in Santa Clara, and finding that their place was infested by cockroaches. Not even the bugs in the Amazon, which they had seen together many years later, had seemed so big to Zane. Ted had given his laugh then too—when they had opened the kitchen cabinet and seen the creatures that could survive so much and live for a week without their head. His laugh had been different back then, Zane actually already knew. It was less refined.

"Less than half an hour, m'lord," Ted said teasingly. "Most of our time was spent trying to find the right cable to connect Lary with the GSD system, truth be told."

Zane smirked.

"Of course it was," he said. "Some things never change… I guess."

Ted smiled. It had been a long time since one of them had cracked that kind of joke.

Zane leaned his back further into the couch and looked around the room. The ceiling was high, maybe thirty or forty feet, and the walls were made of an alloy that would turn transparent when you walked past it or looked at it at a certain angle. Behind the far wall and the two side ones were the habitats of endangered animals. Fish swam over wildcats and birds flew under snakes. The technology had made it possible. The great Egyptian architect-artist who had pitched this room to Zane about a decade ago had envisioned it for his personal office, but Zane had started giggling when he had heard this and said that those animals deserved extinction more than being turned into some ludicrous showcase of 20th century philanthropism for his dick. The architect's eyes had darkened and he'd bowed his head and left without a word. Some years later, Zane had contacted him again and proposed an entire building—no, *campus* for the animals. A proper home for them while the company and other organizations cleaned up the planet. The artist had immediately agreed. One year later, exactly to the day, construction had been completed and the master had hung his head down low again and left the building weeping, "It is my greatest work!"

This was just one of the four (technically, five) lobbies that they were sitting/standing in. It was utterly quiet other than the sound of their breathing.

Zane cleared his throat. He looked at Ted again. Ted asked, "Did you hear about Adam Seranos?"

Zane nodded his head. "I found out this morning. Before coming here, actually." He couldn't help but smile again. Adam had stepped down from his company—one of Zane and Ted's main competitors—and the personal archnemesis to Zane himself. Not because he was an asshole. Quite the opposite. Adam was so honest and kind in his work and life that Zane couldn't help but fight him (honorably, of course; for the most part). He was too much of an inspiration not to. The main one, if Zane was being honest.

"Riley Mahone took his place."

"Yeah," Zane said. His eyes smiled up at Ted. He knew that Ted had always had a crush on her. Zane wouldn't mind bedding her himself.

"Do you think sentimental old age finally got him?"

Ted's eyes looked away, and he thought for a moment. "No."

Zane was already nodding his head up and down. He breathed in. "Well, Ted, thank you as always." He made a slight move forward as if to get off the couch—but he stopped himself midway, so that his back was still almost completely touching the cushion behind him except for the small of his neck.

"I'll see you tomorrow?" he said.

"Yeah," Ted said. "I'll see you tomorrow, man."

"Alright."

Ted turned and walked across the room. His footsteps were the perfect combination of loud and unobtrusive. The metal doors slid open for him. They exhaled lightly and closed behind him.

Zane breathed out and let himself go fully back on the couch again. He lay his head up on the black cushion and looked up at the ceiling.

'So…' he thought. '2,000,506,892 people would have to die in order for the Top 5 companies to stay in business, and not be bought out by the UN or more likely one of the other five conglomerates rapidly healing the world's oceans and purifying the air and regenerating the earth. Give or take a couple tens of thousands.'

The cockroaches in the ceiling were beginning to get into formation again. There were millions of them. In a few seconds they were spelling out the company words again, "Anything Can Change"

Zane looked at the words and the cockroaches for sixty seconds and then the bugs began to move off again and return to more natural movements. They scuttled quickly and slowly, at their own pace. As always.

Zane looked up at the ceiling for a few more seconds, and then he moved his head forward and got off the couch. He started walking around the couch to the doors on the other end of the room and out the lobby. He went to go see his family, probably.

!!!

Hey

                    Jesus Christ it's
                    been 40 years

34*

                    Hey
                    Whatever
                    How are you?

How are you?

                    I'm okay

I'm good

                    I guess we both
                    survived the
                    apocalypse, huh?

I'm happy you're
alive

                    I'm glad you're
                    alive too

Ouch

                    What?

"Glad"?

                    Yeah, glad

Ok

                    What?

Nothing. How are you
How's your family?

We're ok. My kids are
alive, but my wife
didn't make it.

Hbu?

I'm sorry

Thank you

My daughter's dead.
Some friends, obviously.
Everyone else is fine

I'm so sorry

It's ok

What was her name?

My wife?

Yeah

Francine.
You didn't know that?

Mm

Why would I know
that?

                        Well…

Because you're a rich
and famous artist?
What? Does it say it
on your Wikipedia or
something?

                        Well… yeah

Mm

                        Why'd you text me?

They turned the phones
back on. I'm texting
a lot of people

                        Also how's your life? Your
                        family? What'd you do for
                        work?

                        Yeah but why ME?

Everything's fiiine
I had a few different
careers, ig. Social work,
Intl. Peace Corps,
coding, painting.
I'm a teacher now

                                That's great.
                                That sounds wonderful.
                                I'm happy for you

Thanks

                                …Can I see one of your
                                paintings?

UGH

                                What?!

NOTHING's changed

                                GREAT

Fuck you

                                Fuck you too baby

                                I miss you

I miss you too

open attachment

                                Wait, this is beautiful

Thank you
Really?

Yeah, really

This is one of the best
paintings I've ever seen

And I'm not even seeing it
in person yet

Stooop

I'm serious.

Thankyou

How come you're not a
famous painter?
Or are you?

Nah!
Don't need that.
Don't want it

Ok

I thought about it for a
bit. But it's just never
really pulled me. If
that makes sense

Fair enough.
I could do w/o the fame
myself

How's your little sister?

Dead.
How's yours?

          Same.

          Let's not talk about our
          families

Yea

          It's good to hear from you.
          I'm glad you text me

I'm glad too

Do you ever wish we
could be together again?

          Yes

Do you want to call?

          That didn't go so well last
          time

I know, I'm sorry.

          I'm sorry too

          It was so awkward lol

YEAH LOL

It really was

But it was nice

                              It was

                              "I love you"

"Mmm, say it again"

                              I love you
                              I'm in love with you

…I love you too

                              Did you listen to Lorde's
                              last album?

Yes

I thought of you

                              I thought of you

:)

I like your books btw
I loved "The Discovery
of Magic"
I read it to my kids
when they were little

Are you crying?

                              Yes

I'm sorry if my writing
ever hurt you

It's ok. I forgive you.

I really miss her

I know

You know the first book I
ever wrote was about you?
I didn't publish it,
obviously

What was it called?

It was called…

The Angel Who Took My
Virginity

JUST KIDDING

You're so STUPID
Idjit

Ahahahahaha
Ha

No, it was called First

Mm

Do you think this will
be the last time we talk?

                        I don't know

Ok…
I should sleep

                        Me too

R u still looking at
your phone?

                        Yes

I'm sorry.
Thank you.
I love you.

That's the last text you
sent me. back in 2022.
Do you remember?

                        Yes

I'm sending it back

I'm sorry
Thank you
I love you

                     I love you too

Good night, Dave

                     Gah ny

Ohlone Parking Garage

On my last day in Fremont, I got a text from my friend William who I had not heard from in a few months. I had met him several years ago in our first year of college together, right here in our hometown's community college. We took Intro to Acting together at the NUMMI theater located in the Smith Center on the Fremont campus of the college. We both took it to fulfill one of our elective units, not being enthusiastic at all about the prospect of being around a bunch of theater kids (that I think neither one of us missed very much from our respective high schools), but we got lucky and that spring semester the class was full of people who were first-time actors and certainly weren't looking to pursue a disastrous career in that crazy direction. (It seemed like half the people I knew growing up wanted to become some sort of 'artist' when they were older. They wanted to be rich and famous and loved by millions in a field that they didn't seem to hold much talent in and honestly, didn't seem to have much of a desire for if one was to take a bit of a closer look. Wasn't life enough for these people? Did they not realize like I did after I left Ohlone that we are all artists in one incomprehensibly large and complex and original and intense and unified masterwork? I don't know. I worry about these people with big dreams. I almost always have. I just want to grab any stupid boy or silly girl by the shoulders who talks big—the younger the more so—and tell them, "Live! Live! That is all you need to do! Can do! Ahhh!!!")

Please excuse my parenthetical emotion. I find that I am filled with a great deal of power and emotion on this last day (for some time, at least) in my birth town. As these thoughts and feelings are expressed into words for you to understand, I cannot promise that what is inside of me will not go too far.

I return to my friend, William, who I have just mentioned I met in my TD-110 Introduction to Acting class. We were both 19 (in fact, we were born just a day apart from each other at Washington Hospital in December of 1999—which we did not find out until much later on, well after the course in the black box theater had ended), and almost from the beginning I could tell that Will… was different. I cringe a little as I use that word, but what am I do when the word is true?

He actually wasn't there that first day, on the Monday. He appeared on Wednesday, sitting in the circle we had created in the middle of the stage taking turns introducing ourselves—an exercise, incidentally, I have always hated, even as a cheerful young child, but the Intro class was the one exception and I couldn't help but fall in love with these characters right on the spot as they introduced themselves, one at a time, some with false shyness, others with true confidence, some with pleasant comedic timing, others who it was obvious they had been carrying the whole angst of their being for more years than they had been alive even—and then there was William, sitting in the right 'corner' of the circle from my position near center stage right (his chair was a little moved back from the group, but only slightly), sitting as if he had always been a part of our little community college company. Weeks later, when he had mentioned to Sarah that he was so glad he had decided to add the class late, and showed up on the second day, Sarah had gone, "What? You were here on the first day." "Uh, no I wasn't," William had said. "Yes you were!" Sarah had said. "Yeah! I saw you come in!" Mo had said. "Yeah!" "For sure." "What're you talkin' about Will?" "You weren't here the first day?" our teacher Michael had said, slowly scratching the side of his white beard. "Nah!"

The class damn near tore him apart. It looked like a mob was surrounding him, like something from an Arthur Miller play. Finally, I stepped in. (Well, voiced in. I stayed seated in the third row up in the stands and just sort of raised my hand and started speaking without being called on.) I told them that he wasn't there on the first day, and that I noticed him for the first time sitting in the circle as we were all introducing ourselves. Everyone stared at me a little dumbfounded— even William himself I now remember with a laugh! If anyone had turned around to look at him at that moment and the expression he was wearing on his face they would have turned right back to me and called me a, "Liar!" To this day, I think the only thing that saved Will and I from getting lynched by our classmates was Timmy walking back into the room with a whole watermelon in his arms and saying, "Hey You guys wanna see me cut this watermelon with some cards!" We did indeed want to see that, so we followed Timmy out of the theater and into the lobby of the Smith Center (and outside to the patio on the gentle insistence of our teacher Michael) where we saw Timmy put the fruit onto a foldable table that was already out there for some reason (I feel like Timmy wasn't the one to put it there) and he took about ten large steps back sort of saddling the air and the ground and turned and began throwing the cards at the watermelon. Most of them sliced into the big fruit and stayed there (someone connected to their Bluetooth speaker and started playing "Eye of the Tiger"). It was quite glorious. As we had been shuffling out of the theater into the small L-shaped passageway that led up into the lobby, Will and I had been at the back of the class and he had whispered to me, "Thank you," and I whispered back, "No problem."

Anyhow, William was a lousy actor. I mean, I've seen some terrible, life-crumpling performances in my time—but Will took the cake and ate it too. I remember for one of the our first assignments, we had to choose and memorize a monologue to perform in class (a classic and good step in any introductory acting class, no matter the age of the its students—it's only right), and on the day of giving the monologues Will walked into class late with the look of absolute death on his face. I almost got out of my usual chair by the door (on the second row) to go help him to his seat. He looked utterly lost. When it was time to pull the numbered, concentric sticks to decide on the order of the monologues (a quite elementary tactic in my opinion but it looked like the mature Michael had taken these doctor 'ahhh' sticks out from a nostalgic drawer containing items and loose papers from his early days in teaching specially for this occasion; I got the impression that he didn't use these sticks for just any set of spring semester students).

We all pulled our sticks from Michael's hands as he walked up and down the stands to each of us, and everybody looked immediately at what number they had gotten save Will. I saw Will look around at everyone looking at their numbers and the sometimes unusual coloring/staining of the light wood over the years, and then finally I saw him turn his stick over and close his eyes and give a deep, tragic, silent sigh. He was fifth. (I heard Timmy shout out, "I got 92!")

One, two, three, four; Will got up from his seat and went down onto the floor of the stage. He had his hands clasped tightly together and his eyes weren't looking at any of us. Then suddenly he looked up and opened his mouth as if to begin and I hear Michael go, "Will…" Will looked at him confused for a moment, and then he realized his mistake and said, 'Right, right,' and started walking out the room. (Michael wanted us to practice entering the room as if this was a real theater audition. 'Oh, yeah,' I thought to myself, completely forgetting that the first four students had done exactly this.) As Will went out the door he turned and said, "Sorry!" to seemingly no one because he looked across the stage to the empty stage left wall (well, there was a medieval-looking mannequin there by a wooden crate/box on the floor, and I thought the dummy took the apology quite gracefully, although not exactly in stride). As the door was slowly swinging closed behind him Michael said, "It's alright, man. It's alright," in his soothing voice.

Not a second later Will burst through the door and started talking to us about his morning. He was talking so quickly that we could barely understand him although his enunciation was oddly on point and then all of a sudden when he got to the center of the stage his speech slowed down terribly and we thought he was having a stroke. He was able to return his speaking to a normal pace however and ended his monologue by saying something about a hair being in his bowl of cereal 'but was it in the bowl? The cereal box? The milk? Or my hair? Was it even there? Nobody knows.' He gave the beat Michael had instructed us to give before ending our audition piece and then he looked up at us and said, "Thank you," and he turned instinctively to the mannequin as he was walking out of the room and said, "Thank you…" He left the room. A second later before waiting for the door to close he walked back in. He returned to the center of the stage and looked up at the audience again and awaited his notes.

After a moment, I heard Michael say, "Will… That's not your monologue."

Will looked at him. He blinked.

"It could be," he said.

Michael slightly repositioned himself in his seat (which was a little higher up in the stands from all of us). "You chose a monologue, didn't you?"

"Yes," Will said, smiling and pointing at Michael. "I did that."

"Which one did you choose?"

(Will had to think about this one for a moment.)

"The first one," he said, pointing both of his index fingers up into the air now. (Most people had chosen the first one.)

"Did you memorize it?" Michael asked.

Will dropped his hands down. "I tried," he said.

"Hmmm…" Michael went.

As if on a hunch, but not a cruel one at all by any means (though probably a slightly humorous one), Michael leaned forward and said, "Could you give us the first line?"

We all turned to look back at Will. The expression he bore on his face was one that said, 'Oh, shit.'

Will cleared his throat and looked down. "Yeah," he said. We could barely hear him. He cleared his throat again, more violently this time and probably damaging his voice more. "Yeah," he repeated, nodding his head and moving his body forward and back as if he was getting ready to jump. (I leaned back tightly into my seat.)

With an intake of breath Will looked up—and said, "I don't remember it."

Michael said, "That's alright, man. That's alright. It's cool. I'll give you the first few words," he said. He repositioned in his seat again and looked intently down at Will. He cleared his throat quite adequately (I thought this an unnecessary flex on the poor thespian, but he probably didn't entirely mean it as one), and said, "I was walking down the street in my neig—"

"The man came running down the pipe—"

Michael raised a hand to stop him. He started again. "I was walking down the street in my neighborhood one day, when I saw—"

"The moon was going around for another drink when it shmashed him on the head and he realized he could see stars—"

Michael gave a terrible sigh and leaned back in his chair, for I think he knew like all of us that Will wasn't doing this on purpose.

Without raising his buried face from his hand Michael muttered (quite articulately, still), "I was walking down the street in my neighborhood one day, when I saw a white—"

" 'Great show,' I cried! The people were dancing around in a mass and praying to nothing as the moon got the pipe and the man sploo!"

"You can sit down, Will."

"Thank you, comrade."

Will went to his seat and we all reeled from the event and blew air from our cheeks and some of us mouthed the word, 'sploo' to ourselves.

Incidentally three out of the four people who had gone before Will had done that first monologue.

This was going to be a difficult semester for Michael.

Somehow or other, me and Will got through the entire semester without ever being paired for anything. We were never scene partners, we never did an acting exercise together, hell, we didn't even run into each other at the bathroom at the same time. I'm surprised the rest of the class didn't think we hated each other. Though, come to think of it, they probably didn't even notice. Things were so airy, or so breezy, or what wind have you that semester in Intro with Will in the class.

Allow me to paint a little mural, a little mid-film montage—a little time-lapse—of what the rest of the semester was like:

During scenes, Will would almost never say his lines correctly, or if he did, he would deliver them in completely the wrong way. For example, in a scene from *Proof* by David Auburn, in which he was playing the character of Harold (Hal) Dobbs opposite Amanda who played the protagonist, Catherine, he had to essentially lie to Catherine for the entire scene because he had secretly stolen one of the notebooks of Catherine's recently deceased father (played by the incomparable 'volcano' Anthony Hopkins in the film adaptation, which I did not watch because I was a good theater student for the duration of those four months and also I was dissuaded from executing the rental upon taking a whiff of its rotten tomatoes [oh, goodness, it's not as stinky as I remember it being—I shall proceed to throw the overly overripe fruits at myself]). At the very end of the scene, Hal is supposed to be leaving Catherine's house and is walking towards the door to exit, when Catherine notices he has forgotten his bag and goes to grab it for him. When she picks it up, her dead father's notebook falls from it and hits the floor. When Will and Amanda went up to go do this scene, before Amanda could finish saying her first line Will had already gotten the bag and handed her the notebook. (Timmy nearly died from his tight inner/outer laughter. Which was a laugh that sort of tightened his insides and all of his outer body until it hopefully—God-willing got out of his mouth past his toothy grin as he had his legs stretched out and his arms crossed and his head tipping to the side; actually, no, What am I saying? That time it erupted out of him like a cackle with his head thrown back.) Later in the course, when we were doing scenes with larger groups, Will and his group mates had chosen a scene from "Something Convenient", a wonderful little short play by William Saroyan, and very intelligently I thought they chose a scene with only three characters in it (there were four people in their group, including Will; Michael looked the other way). All Will had to do was stand behind Juan and Rupashi as they grilled Enrique's character, and maybe ad-lib a few lines if he wanted to, but when the characters who actually existed in the scene settled their differences and were about to commemorate their new friendship with a few touching words and perhaps a firm hand on the shoulder, Will walked straight past Juan and Rupashi and slapped Enrique in the face. Another day Will walked late into class with a three-piece blue and white velvet suit on for some reason as Michael was talking to us, and we all turned to look at him and quite couldn't believe how good he looked, and Michael went, "You're upstaging me, man." "Oh," said Will. And he looked and started unbuckling his belt and Michael and all of us went, "No, no, no, no!" and reached in to stop him. (Although quickly afterwards some of the girls in the class and a few of the guys whispered to each other, 'Did we really need to stop him?') And then there was this other day, I'll never forget it for as long as I live, where we were all out on the floor of the stage about to do some warm-up that Michael was visibly very excited about, when he noticed that Will and Jeremy were in the back of our little crowd joking around and talking it up as Michael was trying to explain the exercise to us. At first he ignored them, thinking that they would eventually quiet down or someone would shush them, but the more and more he tried to explain the activity the louder and louder Will and Jeremy got (the rest of us had become dead silent—I had never seen Michael get this angry, before or since). Suddenly Will burst out into laughter, and Michael snapped. "Alright. You know what? Forget about the warm-up. Will?"

"Yeah?"

"Here's what I want you to do. I want you to walk from that end of the stage," (he pointed), "to that end." (He pointed to the other end.) "Stage left to stage right. You think you can do that for us?"

"Yeah," Will said happily. "For sure."

He walked over to stage left. He turned around.

"In a straight line."

Will looked up at Michael. He stared at him. Michael stared back. (We shot furtive glances back between teacher and student.)

Will looked back down again at the stage. "For sure, for sure…" he said more quietly. He took a breath. He put one foot forward. (We all moved back a little to give him plenty of space. He glanced back up at Michael to see if he was acting. He was not.) He took another step forward. And then another, and then another. And then slowly but surely, he got to the other end of the stage. He stood there at the other end of the stage for a moment, in front of the black curtains on wing two or three, with his back turned to us, and just as I was about to call, "Will?" he began to faint. We all rushed to stage right to catch him. (He slept peacefully for the rest of the period. When he woke up

Michael told him he didn't have to come to class on Friday, but Will came. I think he knew we wouldn't truly be Intro without him.)

On the last day of class, and the last day of the spring semester, we had a little potluck right here in the NUMMI. Attendance was optional, as there was no more about acting that Michael could teach us or critique us on in this beginning level course, but everybody still came much to everybody else's delight and relief I think. It was a little awkward at first, all of us hanging around and talking to each other and walking freely around the stage and backstage for the entire period without any guidance at all from Michael, but pretty quickly every one forgot about the strangeness of us being together again one last time in this space and everyone got along quite fine and happily as the music played in the background. By the end of it, I think, everybody was really relishing everybody else's company and nobody wanted to leave and return to their inhibitions waiting patiently for them in the lobby (some maybe even hiding quite menacingly in the dim passageway that led up to it). At one point, somebody dropped something in the stands (I think it was Andrea, but I can't be sure), and it fell through one of the openings between rows and I was relieved to have something specific to do. I went in from stage left and crawled around, quite afraid there would be an earthquake at this time with my luck or the stands would simply shut closed like some miniature toy and the thin rectangular bars would take me with them and snap my body. But, Will was in there with me (he had entered from stage right—well, I suppose this would be house left and right), and with him crawling around on all fours with me looking for the thing and getting our pants and palms dirty beyond belief and inhaling some rather interesting scents, I somehow felt safer. I felt that nothing too awful would happen to me here in this dark place under the NUMMI seats while Will was with me.

Finally, we got out, with no success, and some time later I would ask Will what had been dropped/what were we looking for and he couldn't remember either.

Right before time ran out, Michael had all of us return to our seats and he shut off the music and he proceeded to give us one last time a brief talk before we all went our separate ways. (Everyone was in a good mood grade-wise too, by the way, because everyone had passed the class—*EVEN* Will, who Michael had gone up to earlier in the week and said, "Yeah, normally I would have to fail someone like you… But I have to say your uh, complete disregard for the writing and the directions in this class, actually managed to bring out some of the best, most truthful performances out of your classmates. So, I guess what I'm trying to say is, Will… You get a B.") Michael thanked everyone for a great semester, and said that groups like ours ('Ones with a complete lack of talent?' I thought) were the reason he loved teaching so much. He also added that he genuinely saw improvement from each and every one of us, and, he stopped, as if he was about to choke on his own words; and Will's hand that shot up was like a Heimlich that saved his life, and he quickly called on Will. "Yes, Will?"

"Yeah, so…" Will began. We all looked at him.

"Wait... I forgot—Oh yeah, yeah. So I've been think-ing... like, all these different characters and stories we've come across in this class... I can't help but keep thinking they're all like trying to figure out the best way to live—even if they don't realize that's what they're doing—and like, some of them do bad things. Some of them do good things. Some of them—a lot of them make mistakes and that's where a lot of the conflict comes in, and a few of them seem to get it right, although I can't really remember which. And like, all of us here in Intro, most of us this is our first year of college, and I feel like we're all also figuring out what the best way to live is, and we all have our own idea of what that is." (At this point Michael's hand was well onto the side of his face and his eyes looked concerned and his mouth was open as if he was about to say something—) "So I guess my question is... What's the best way to live?"

Nobody said anything for a smooth minute. We all looked at Michael, whose head was down and his hand was up to his chin in a much calmer pose of thought than I expected (I shot a glance over at Will—he looked like he wanted to kill himself).

Finally, after one-and-a-half minutes of silent contem-plation, Michael looked back up at Will, and said, "Live. Just live. That's the only way... I think."

Will nodded his head, processing what Michael had just said to him. He looked back up.

"Alright," he said, leaning a little bit back in his chair. "I'll try."

"Ah!" Michael said. "There is no—"

'Yeah, yeah,' we all said, nodding our heads and looking away. After a beat, Timmy in the back went, "That's right Michael!" then he let out his shrill guffaw, tapping one foot loudly once, then twice on the stands.

Michael looked up at him with murder on his face. He stared at Timmy. Then he let out his deep, rapid giggle: "Eheh-heh-heh-heh-heh,"

After class ended, we all entered the lobby, still talking and joking around with each other, not wanting to leave, and then Fred and Jasper and them had to come kindly kick us out because they and The Entertainment Arts Guild (God, I'm so glad they ended up changing their club name later) had to dress up the lobby for an event that night. We all exited the building, and continued our conversations outside on the patio area. Finally, I was getting ready to be the first one to leave and was dreading being the inevitable catalyst that would finally cause us to all break apart, when suddenly Will came up to me and asked, "Hey, you said you don't like boba, right?" I nodded my head; this was indeed true. Will said, "I think I found a drink you might like." He started for the long staircase that led down and away from the Smith Center. "Follow me!" he said, and we both slipped away without anybody noticing—or so I thought. At the bottom of the stairs, I sensed some sort of shadow over us and I turned to see the entire class standing at the top of the stairs and pushing each other a little for room. They were all there: Amanda, Juan, Rupashi, Enrique, Jeremy, Andrea, Timmy, Mo, Sarah, Sabrina, DJ, Yorick, Ana, Hein, Oscar, Kelly, Mahmoud, Kevin, Harsh, Roberto Ramon Escobar Castillo III (if that really is your REAL name). Oh, and Ri. They all looked down at us and called loudly and obnoxiously their goodbyes and we waved and smiled back at them and I felt the lump catch in my throat. I quickly turned away and we headed to Will's car (a 2006 silver Toyota RAV4); it was parked in the staff parking lot which was definitely closer to the NUMMI than the students'. 'Do you always park here?' I almost asked, but based on the smile we shared as Will was about to unlock the car I think I had my answer.

We drove to CAFFE:iN over in Union City, which, I had obviously never been to, and there I had my first sip of honeydew milk tea which, I indeed, very much liked. Will got one for himself, and I asked him if he had ever watched the sunset from the top floor of the Ohlone parking garage. He said he hadn't, and this kind of amazed me. He drove us back to campus up Mission Boulevard (or, well, I guess it was *down* Mission Boulevard, but it always feels like up to me, no matter the direction we're coming from), and we parked up at the top floor (my own car was a few levels down) and we made the honeydew milk teas last the entire time until sunset and we watched the big star go down over the Bay and Will marveled at the sight. I wanted to tell him to stop looking so long at the sun, but I didn't. Finally once the stars were out to take our place and other people had come to take in the view and smoke weed and make out, Will and I parted ways and suddenly I realized how badly I needed to use the bathroom. I never had much luck finding an open restroom on campus after dark so I just leapt down the stairs not even thinking to try the elevator and rushed to my car unlocked it and drove home. As I was trying not to speed too much and hit a deer or a skunk on the road I thought to myself how easy it was to talk to Will, and how quickly those hours until sunset had passed. He was the first and only person I've ever met who found everything I was saying genuinely interesting. Not even my own mother or future true love (if ever I find them) could ever put up with me talking so much about all the different things I had just talked about with Will. Not even my own self could have withstood such a thing! (If anybody is interested, we mostly talked about video games [namely *Assassin's Creed* and *Kingdom Hearts*] and movies [mostly ones by Christopher Nolan, although I also expressed my abject disappointment in the M.C.U. and also though it's obviously not a movie *Game of Thrones*]; actually, come to think of it, I expressed great disappointment in all of the above. They all lasted too long, I thought. Or they weren't being genuine anymore. Will agreed with me on most of my points I think, but he said he couldn't help but love when stories ended up sabotaging themselves. He had a wide grin on his face. He said it reminded him of people—and of himself. 'Huh,' is all I said to that, not knowing what else to say. [It was deep, for sure.] No, no, he hadn't said 'sabotage,' he had said something else. He used some other word. Or phrase. Oh, what was it? What was it?! I can't remember… Destroy? Had he said 'destroy themselves'? I became grave at the thought of it.) Suddenly the pain in my body returned and I pushed on the gas harder.

I was looking forward to hanging out with Will again, to hear his thoughts again on different things and to have a new friend in my life again who took every serious word I said seriously and every joking word with levity (I realized it had been a long time since I had that type of friendship with somebody, with a peer, I suppose), and I think my hanging out with Will was also a way for me to continue having the energy of Intro in my life even though the class had already ended. Of course, this energy didn't really last, Will and I's conversations became more and more strained, we saw each other less and less, and finally the last time we saw each other we were getting breakfast at our usual spot Country Way, and we were both late and we had barely anything to say to each other and by the time we parted ways I was feeling quite depressed. Another friend had come and gone in my life, I thought, when I was thinking that Will would be one to last (we even started calling each other 'brother' and said we'd be the best man at each other's weddings, though Will was almost one-hundred percent sure he'd never get married and honestly this kinda made me relieved for his imaginary future-fiancé), and as I sat in my car in the tiny parking lot of the diner I thought to myself yet again here was a person I had hung out too much with. I had taken it too far. Turned a good thing into a bad. Turned giving into taking. And what made it all the more depressing was the knowledge that Will had more to give me but I was the one who was all out of energy for our relationship. I closed my eyes and put a hand to my head, and I vowed that I would never go too far in another one of my relationships again.

I was driving up Pine Street to see him now. It was mid-late afternoon on a Sunday in early March. The weather outside was sunny but cool, and it had been quite gloomy in the morning when it seemed like the sun would stay forgotten behind the clouds for the entire day. I took a nap before coming here—a proper nap, less than thirty minutes long—and I had woken up feeling really refreshed and energetic after all the last-minute packing for my move tomorrow. I had opened my eyes suddenly to see the sunlight coming in through the blinds which I had not bothered to close before going to sleep, thinking it unnecessary with all the gray gloom outside, and I had smiled and stretched out my body on my childhood and young adulthood bed and breathed out noisily. I turned my head to the TV dinner table I was using as a bedside table, and reached for my phone knowing in me somewhere that there was in important notification to check. It was Will. He wanted to meet up at the Ohlone parking garage and watch the sunset with me. 'One last time.'

As I was driving up the hill, I remembered these last words in his text and I began to worry a little. What did he mean, 'one last time'? Was he moving away like me? Was he planning on never going back there for some reason? Was he depressed? These thoughts came one after the other and all at once and none of them seemed to be true in this case, so they slipped away almost as easily as they had come. I myself had been to Ohlone a number of times after I transferred to SF State. I liked visiting and walking around the campus, both the Fremont and Newark one, pretending that I was still a student and having every right to enjoy the somewhat subdued environment around me. (I even kept the parking sticker from my last semester there on the windshield of my car, "Spring 2020", which anyone like me who had that barely used because the pandemic had sent us all home). I still came back though, walking around the grounds on my own, not talking to anyone, and for some reason my mind would always be totally clear when I came here. I walked the dirt path to the three benches on Newark campus, a spot Marisela had revealed to me when we were working on a group video for our Spanish class back in our second semester at Ohlone, looking out into the expanse and the mountains in the distance, a place where I had later taken a coworker to during the first year of the pandemic and she laughed at me when I had asked her if those mountains in the distance were the Sierra Nevadas. I still don't really know. There was also a really good statue of Native Americans that they had put in on the Fremont campus, and I would stare at it in contemplation, the irony not lost on me.

Not a month went by after I transferred where I hadn't been back, evening begging my mom—no—*demanding* she Venmo some money for gas so that I could drive all the way from SF to go back there one day. It had been a long time though since I had been back at the parking garage, I just realized. I tried remembering when was the last time, but then I spotted Will's dirty RAV4 up at the edge of the top floor, framed against the blue and a bit of white sky. It was dirtier than ever. I smiled as I drove up the last bit of the incline and around the edge that led to the entrance, and I thought I heard music as I was going up but by the time I reached the entrance I no longer heard it.

I went over the bump, and I slowly curved over to the left, much more slowly than I needed to, I realized, and drove down and to the right where Will's car was parked in the center spot of the parking row up against the wall. I noticed for the first time that he was sitting on top of the SUV, with his long arms wrapped lightly around his legs.

I parked a couple spots down to his right and got out of my car. I walked up to him casually and he turned to me.

"You look like God," I said.

Will laughed.

"Not exactly," he said. "Here, c'mon up here man. The view is incredible!"

Will helped me climb up onto the side of his car, and onto the top of the roof. I was more limber than I expected, but when I sat down on the top right next to him I started panting.

"Those Amazon boxes are making you strong," I said.

Will just turned to me and did an incredible impression of the grating sound Amazon delivery trucks make as they are unintentionally conquering the world.

I laughed, and he laughed, and we turned back towards the view and sat there silently for a few minutes.

I was the one to break the silence.

"I should have brought us some honeydew milk teas before coming here," I said.

Will smiled slightly without looking at me, and said, "That's alright. As long as we remember what they taste like."

I nodded my head firmly in assent.

A few more moments passed. Will turned to me.

"Congratulations on the job, man," he said. "It sounds really cool. Like something you always wanted."

I couldn't help but grin. "Thank you, Will," I said looking down. "Yeah, I'm honestly really excited about it." I looked over at him. "I actually couldn't sleep last night." I started to laugh; he started to laugh, too. "I was so damn excited. I haven't felt this way since I was a kid." I looked at him again suddenly. My smile went away. "I leave tomorrow," I said, glancing away. I looked back at him. He was faced forward again.

"I know," he said, mysteriously.

I was quiet for a moment; and then I said, "Did Simi tell you?"

"Yeah."

He laughed, and I laughed too. 'Mmhmm,' I quietly said, turning back forward again. (I looked around me— there were only a few other cars spotted around us that I could see; less than I thought there would be, even for a Sunday afternoon. I turned back around.)

"Is that why you wanted to hang out?" I asked.

He continued to look forward, trying to catch every detail of the skyline it seemed, and suddenly I started to become anxious.

Will was silent for a second, and then he breathed in. "Noo…," he said. "I actually had a couple questions I wanted to ask you. I wanted to get your thoughts on some things."

I nodded my head.

"Sure," I said. "Shoot." (I closed my eyes briefly with a shade of self-annoyance. Will didn't react.)

"My first question, is… Do you think people change?"

I looked down and thought for a second, though I already knew my answer.

"No." I said. "I used to think they do," (I shifted a little in my position), "but I think we can only change how we behave, not who we are."

Will nodded his head.

"Yeah, I think so too." He continued nodding his head, and he looked away to his left for a bit.

"Hey you want a lollipop?" he said.

"No," I said, almost laughing. "Why? Do you have one?"

"No," he said, smiling and looking down. The way he did it almost broke me.

"What's your second question?" I asked gently.

He continued looking down. He pursed his lips and his cheeks flexed a little from the grinding of his teeth.

"I only have one more question," he said. He raised his head. "If we can't change who we are, if we can't change our nature…" My breathing was silent. "Should we ever fight our nature?" He looked at me. "Should we ever not be who we are?"

I thought I wanted to break his gaze, but I didn't. I looked at him. Into his eyes.

"No," I said. "I think we should always be true to ourselves…" I was so confident a moment ago, but I found I had more to say. Five more words. "But I can't be sure."

I gave it a beat, and then I was able to look away from Will. My eyes were downcast, and then I looked back up at the view; but I couldn't tell you what I was looking at.

Though I wasn't looking at him anymore, I knew Will was faced forward. Not seeing the same thing that I was seeing.

The minutes passed… but yet we were still so far away from sunset.

My face was contorted a little in feelings, and I turned my head to look at Will again. My mouth opened slightly. I, I didn't…

'I'm sorry,' Will said. He looked at me. I looked at him. I looked into his amber eyes.

"Don't be," I found myself saying. The clouds started to come back again, and I thought I heard thunder, but it must have been my imagination.

Sound and some color disappeared for a moment, and I thought I saw lightning flash across Will's face, but I turned and I saw that it was the sun just going behind a cumulus. I turned back to Will.

"Aram."

I stared at him. The fear was very real now.

"Do you think things will be any different, the next time around?"

Suddenly "Waltz" by Khachaturian began blasting on the speaker of the car. The violins soared and the drums and cellos climbed in the fourth movement.

The world around us started to get darker, and over the music I heard people walking up the sidewalk below us to the parking garage shout in confusion. I turned and I saw that some areas of the Bay were brighter than ever. I turned back.

"Do you think that we'll be friends, again? Do you think that we'll exist?"

The music was heightening it was crescendoing into its final act.

I looked at him, but I didn't know what I was looking at anymore.

"I don't know…" I continued looking. I saw something. I let out a gasp. The music stopped.

"Who are you?" I whispered.

Will, my friend, looked at me, and then he looked out at the view, and said:

"I am William H. Yogamoth. I am the Fifth and Final Force of Nature, and I have come to bring things to an end."

The fear went away, and I felt the world coming in closer, or I was coming closer. It was all coming together. The edge of the universe was at my fingertips, the Sun had passed through me so long ago it was as if it was another reality. I'm surprised I even remembered it. I felt everything converging into the singularity. And then, almost at the same time, it seemed…: Big Bang